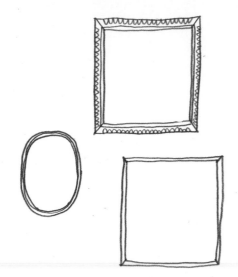

For Louis
& Sophie
JS

Groundwood Books / House of Anansi Press
groundwoodbooks.com

We acknowledge for their financial support of our publishing program
the Canada Council for the Arts, the Ontario Arts Council and
the Government of Canada.

Canada Council
for the Arts

Conseil des Arts
du Canada

ONTARIO ARTS COUNCIL
CONSEIL DES ARTS DE L'ONTARIO
an Ontario government agency
un organisme du gouvernement de l'Ontario

With the participation of the Government of Canada
Avec la participation du gouvernement du Canada | Canadä

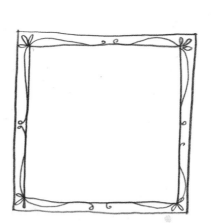

Library and Archives Canada Cataloguing in Publication
Sobol, John, author
Friend or foe / John Sobol ; pictures by Dasha Tolstikova.
Issued in print and electronic formats.
ISBN 978-1-55498-407-7 (bound).—ISBN 978-1-55498-408-4 (pdf)
I. Tolstikova, Dasha, illustrator II. Title.
PS8637.O36F75 2016   jC813'.6   C2015-908423-7
C2015-908424-5

The illustrations are graphite and ink wash on paper, with some digital color.
Design by Michael Solomon
Printed and bound in Malaysia

FSC
www.fsc.org

MIX
Paper from
responsible sources
FSC® C012700

For Sheila B.
DT

FRIEND

or

FOE?

John Sobol

PICTURES BY Dasha Tolstikova

GROUNDWOOD BOOKS
HOUSE OF ANANSI PRESS
TORONTO BERKELEY

THIS is how it was…

A lonely mouse lived in a small house beside a
great palace.
In the great palace lived a cat.

Every evening the mouse crept along the rafters and out onto the roof.

Every evening the cat climbed the stairs to the palace tower and sat in the highest window.

Every night, as darkness settled, the cat peered down at the mouse, and the mouse stared up at the cat.

This is how it was.

The palace had only one entrance, and it was carefully guarded. Nobody entered and nobody left without the queen's permission. Not even the cat.

One day the mouse noticed a tiny hole in the palace wall. He stared at the hole for a whole day. He was wondering if — after all those hours of looking at each other — he and the cat were friends.

The more he thought about it, the more curious he became. Was the cat his friend?

He wanted a friend.

Finally he made up his mind. Slipping quietly out of his house, he squeezed through the tiny hole and into the palace.

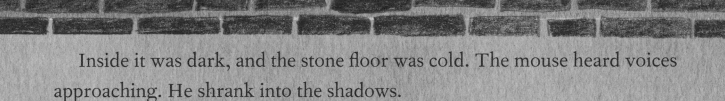

Inside it was dark, and the stone floor was cold. The mouse heard voices approaching. He shrank into the shadows.

People went past wearing glittering robes. Laughing and joking, they didn't see the little mouse at their feet.

As the mouse climbed the stairs to the palace tower, he began to grow afraid.

What if he was wrong? If he was, the cat would tear him to pieces. Still, he kept climbing.

Was the cat friend or foe?

He had to know.

It took all day to climb the stairs. But finally, as the sun was setting, the mouse reached the top step. He peered around the great oak door and there was the cat, sitting on the window sill, staring at the empty rooftop below.

Carefully the mouse crept closer. Silently he climbed the thick velvet curtain by the window. Finally he sat on the stone window sill next to the cat.

The cat was still staring with wide eyes at the house far below, searching for the mouse. She had no idea that he was so near.

At last, gathering all his courage, the mouse
squeaked, "Hello, are you friend or foe?"

The cat whirled around. She spied the mouse and leapt high in the air. She had never been so surprised in all her life!

The mouse studied the cat's whiskered face as she flew through the air. At first he felt sure he was about to be eaten. Then he changed his mind. Perhaps they were to be friends after all.

Friend or foe, thought the mouse. In a moment I'll know.

But as the cat spun to face the mouse, she slipped. The mouse reached out his paw, but it was too late. The cat fell from the window sill.

With wide eyes, the mouse watched the cat fall.

The cat fell with a long howl from the high palace tower. But, being a cat, she landed safely. Outside the palace walls.

A moment later, a woman came out of the small house and scooped up the cat.

"Why, we've been wanting a cat, and now here you are. Dropped right out of the sky, didn't you, puss?"

The woman gave the cat a saucer of milk.
"Stay as long as you like, so long as you get rid of that mouse that creeps along the rafters every night."

A cat lives in a small house beside a great palace. In the great palace lives a mouse.

Every evening the mouse creeps up the stairs
to the palace tower. Every evening the cat climbs
to the roof of the house.

The mouse looks down at the cat. The cat stares up at the mouse.

Every evening the mouse wonders, friend or foe?

And every evening
he sighs.
I don't know.